D1288785

MIGHTY MORPHIN POWER RANGERS

SABAN'S

1

WRITTEN BY
KYLE HIGGINS

ILLUSTRATED BY
HENDRY PRASETYA

COLORS BY
MATT HERMS

LETTERS BY
ED DUKESHIRE

WHAT TIME IS IT?!

WRITTEN BY
MAIRGHREAD SCOTT

ILLUSTRATED BY
DANIEL BAYLISS

LETTERS BY
ED DUKESHIRE

COVER BY
GOÑI MONTES

DESIGNER
JILLIAN CRAB

ASSISTANT EDITOR
ALEX GALER

EDITOR
DAFNA PLEBAN

HASBRO SPECIAL THANKS
BRIAN CASENTINI, MELISSA FLORES, EDGAR PASTEN, PAUL STRICKLAND, MARCY GEORGE, JASON BISCHOFF, ED LANE, BETH ARTALE, AND **MICHAEL KELLY**

 ABDO Spotlight  BOOM! STUDIOS

Licensed by:
 Hasbro

ABDOBOOKS.COM

Reinforced library bound edition published in 2020 by Spotlight,
a division of ABDO, PO Box 398166, Minneapolis, Minnesota 55439.
Spotlight produces high-quality reinforced library bound editions for
schools and libraries. Published by agreement with BOOM! Studios.

Printed in the United States of America, North Mankato, Minnesota.
092019
012020

THIS BOOK CONTAINS
RECYCLED MATERIALS

Licensed by:

Library of Congress Control Number: 2019942386

Publisher's Cataloging-in-Publication Data

Names: Higgins, Kyle, author. | Prasetya, Hendry; Herms, Matt; Silas, Thony;
    Valenza, Bryan; illustrators.
Title: Mighty morphin power rangers/ writer: Kyle Higgins; art: Hendry Prasetya;
    Matt Herms; Thony Silas; Bryan Valenza.
Description: Minneapolis, Minnesota: Spotlight, 2020 | Series: Mighty morphin
    power rangers
Summary: Tommy Oliver was new in town when evil doer, Rita Repulsa, made him
    the Green Ranger. After escaping her mind control, he hopes for a normal life,
    which isn't easy to do with the plights of high school, making new friends, and
    the dangers that come with being a Power Ranger.
Identifiers: ISBN 9781532144233 (#1, lib. bdg.) | ISBN 9781532144240 (#2, lib.
    bdg.) | ISBN 9781532144257 (#3, lib. bdg.) | ISBN 9781532144264 (#4, lib.
    bdg.) | ISBN 9781532144271 (#5, lib. bdg.) | ISBN 9781532144288 (#6, lib.
    bdg.) | ISBN 9781532144295 (#7, lib. bdg.) | ISBN 9781532144301 (#8, lib.
    bdg.) | ISBN 9781532144318 (#9, lib. bdg.)
Subjects: LCSH: Mighty Morphin Power Rangers (Television program)--Juvenile
    fiction. | Ninjas--Juvenile fiction. | Superheroes--Juvenile fiction. | Good and
    evil--Juvenile fiction. | Graphic novels--Juvenile fiction. | Comic books, strips,
    etc.--Juvenile fiction
Classification: DDC 741.5--dc23

Spotlight

A Division of ABDO
abdobooks.com

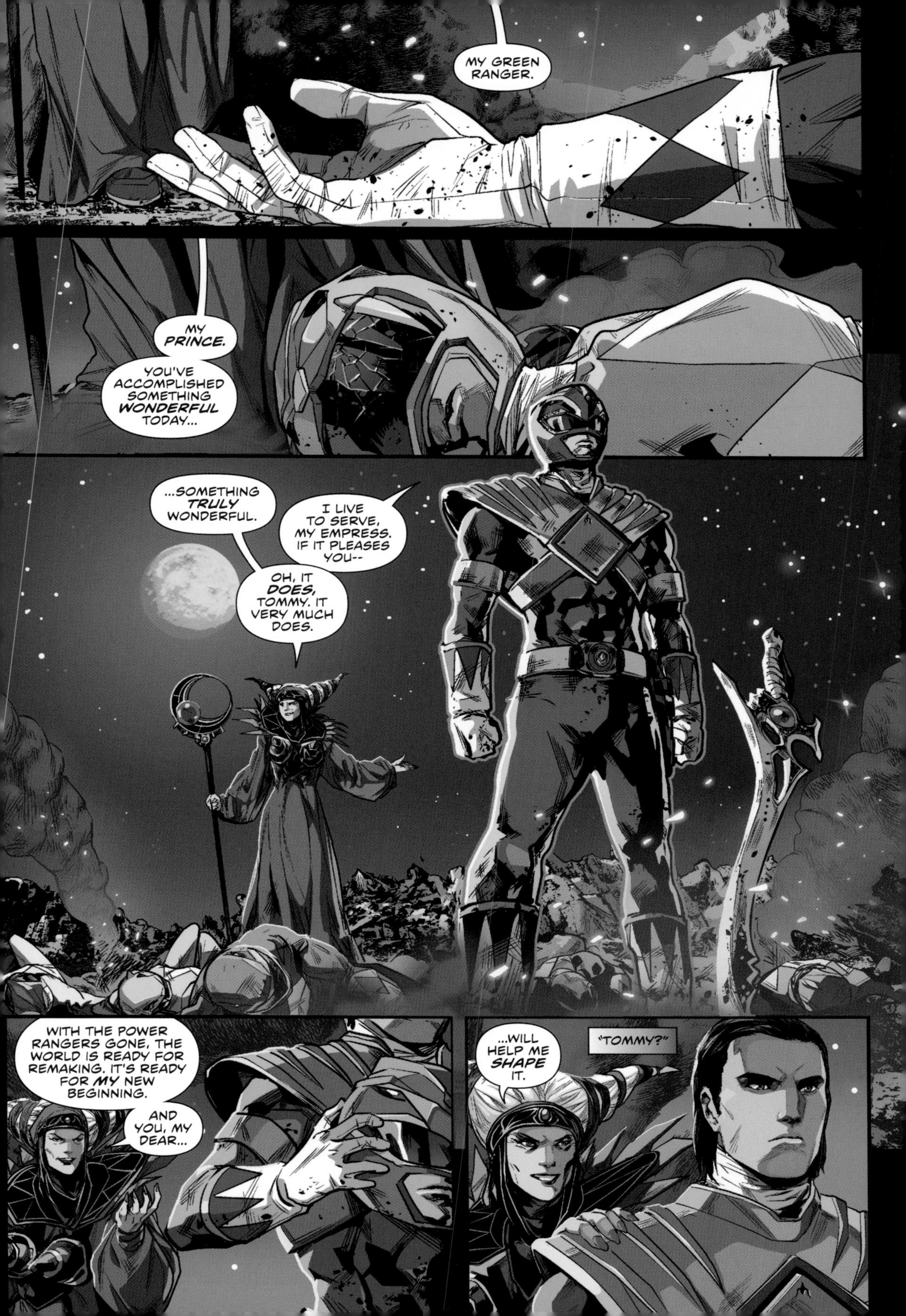
MY GREEN RANGER.
MY PRINCE.
YOU'VE ACCOMPLISHED SOMETHING WONDERFUL TODAY...
...SOMETHING TRULY WONDERFUL.
I LIVE TO SERVE, MY EMPRESS. IF IT PLEASES YOU--
OH, IT DOES, TOMMY. IT VERY MUCH DOES.
WITH THE POWER RANGERS GONE, THE WORLD IS READY FOR REMAKING. IT'S READY FOR MY NEW BEGINNING.
AND YOU, MY DEAR...
"TOMMY?"
...WILL HELP ME SHAPE IT.

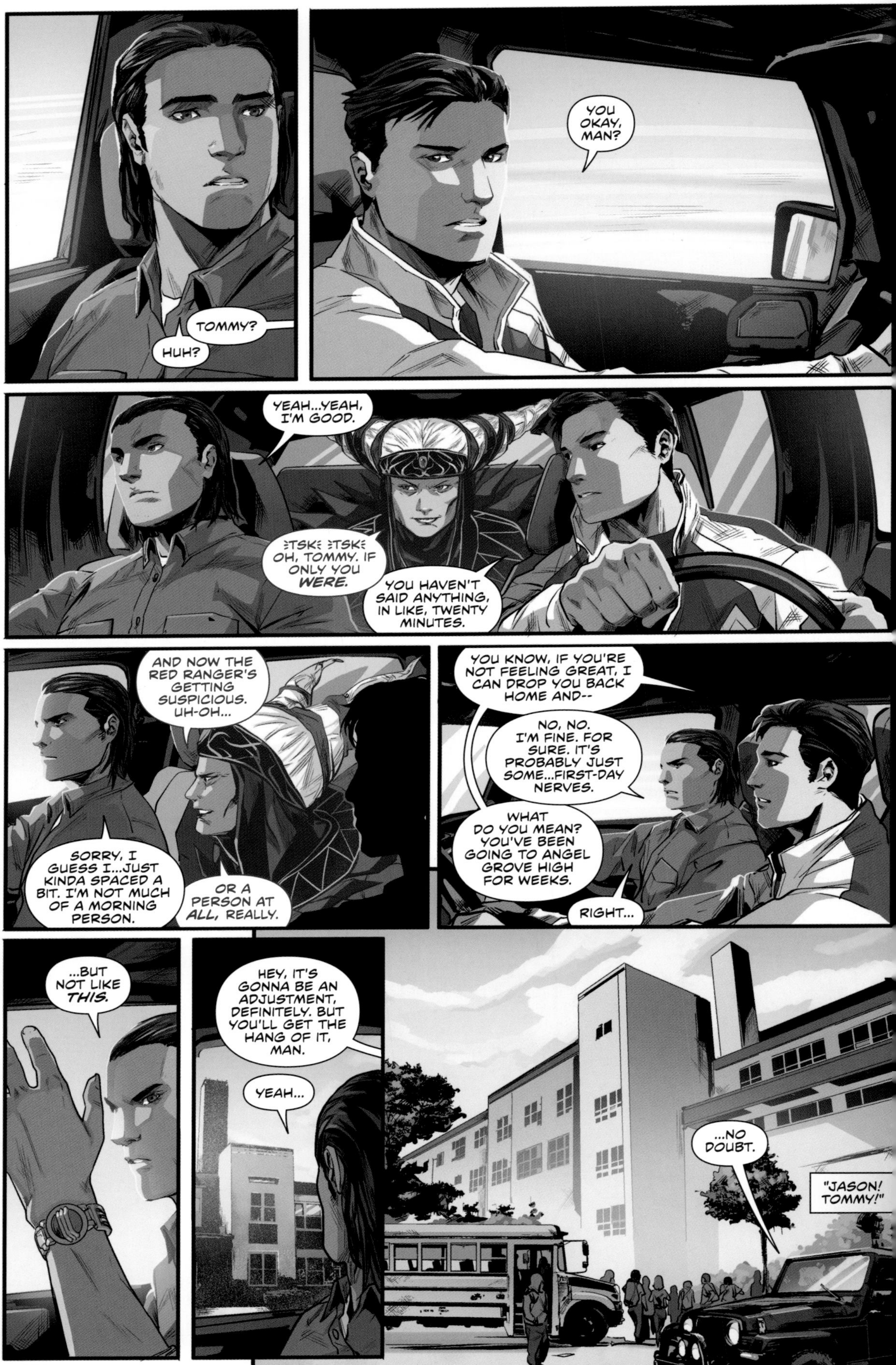
TOMMY?
HUH?
YOU OKAY, MAN?
YEAH...YEAH, I'M GOOD.
TSK TSK OH, TOMMY. IF ONLY YOU WERE.
YOU HAVEN'T SAID ANYTHING, IN LIKE, TWENTY MINUTES.
AND NOW THE RED RANGER'S GETTING SUSPICIOUS. UH-OH...
SORRY, I GUESS I...JUST KINDA SPACED A BIT. I'M NOT MUCH OF A MORNING PERSON.
OR A PERSON AT ALL, REALLY.
YOU KNOW, IF YOU'RE NOT FEELING GREAT, I CAN DROP YOU BACK HOME AND--
NO, NO. I'M FINE. FOR SURE. IT'S PROBABLY JUST SOME...FIRST-DAY NERVES.
WHAT DO YOU MEAN? YOU'VE BEEN GOING TO ANGEL GROVE HIGH FOR WEEKS.
RIGHT...
...BUT NOT LIKE THIS.
HEY, IT'S GONNA BE AN ADJUSTMENT, DEFINITELY. BUT YOU'LL GET THE HANG OF IT, MAN.
YEAH...
...NO DOUBT.
"JASON! TOMMY!"

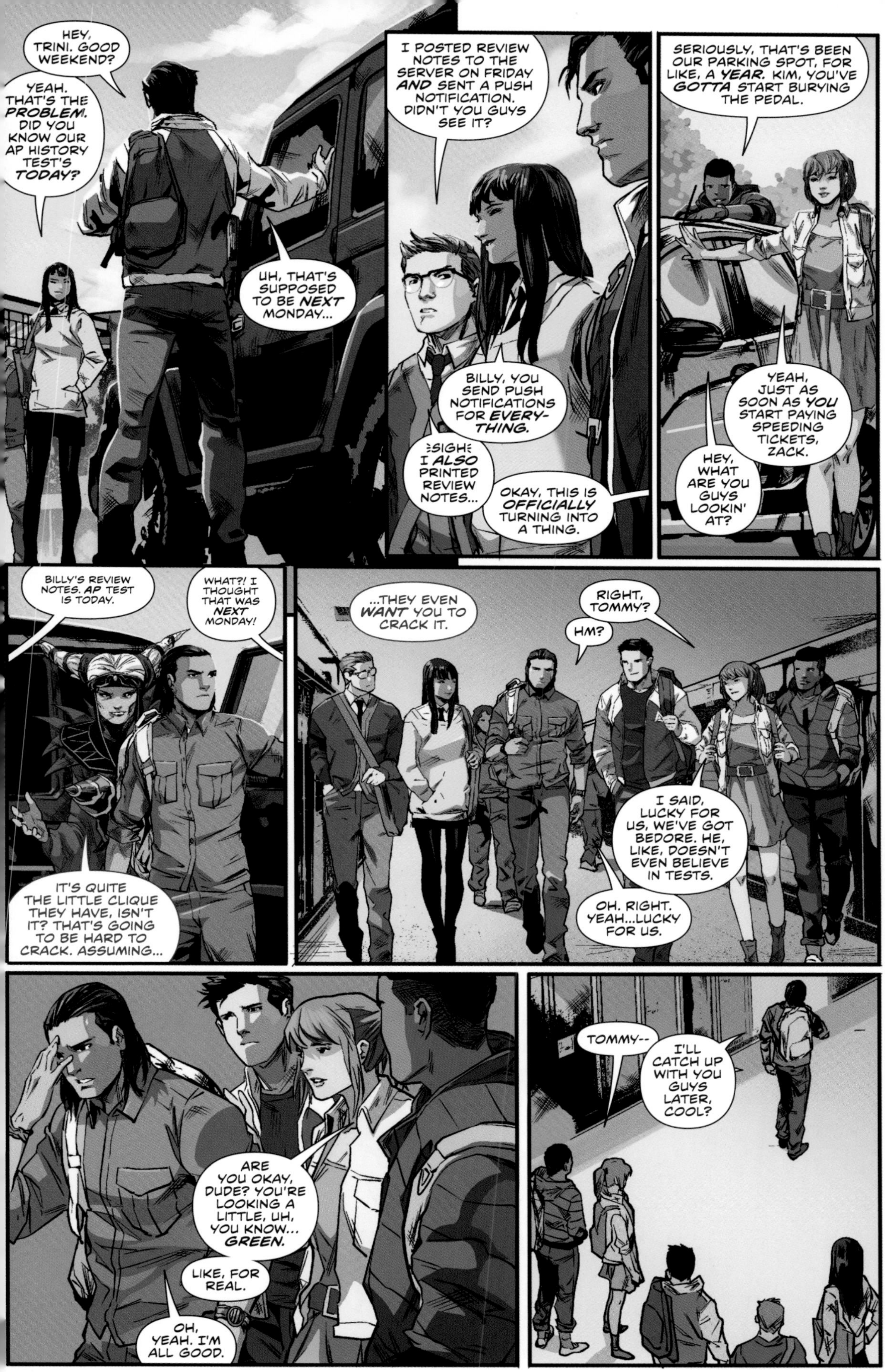
HEY, TRINI. GOOD WEEKEND?
YEAH. THAT'S THE PROBLEM. DID YOU KNOW OUR AP HISTORY TEST'S TODAY?
UH, THAT'S SUPPOSED TO BE NEXT MONDAY...
I POSTED REVIEW NOTES TO THE SERVER ON FRIDAY AND SENT A PUSH NOTIFICATION. DIDN'T YOU GUYS SEE IT?
BILLY, YOU SEND PUSH NOTIFICATIONS FOR EVERY-THING.
SIGH I ALSO PRINTED REVIEW NOTES...
OKAY, THIS IS OFFICIALLY TURNING INTO A THING.
SERIOUSLY, THAT'S BEEN OUR PARKING SPOT, FOR LIKE, A YEAR. KIM, YOU'VE GOTTA START BURYING THE PEDAL.
YEAH, JUST AS SOON AS YOU START PAYING SPEEDING TICKETS, ZACK.
HEY, WHAT ARE YOU GUYS LOOKIN' AT?
BILLY'S REVIEW NOTES. AP TEST IS TODAY.
WHAT?! I THOUGHT THAT WAS NEXT MONDAY!
IT'S QUITE THE LITTLE CLIQUE THEY HAVE, ISN'T IT? THAT'S GOING TO BE HARD TO CRACK. ASSUMING...
...THEY EVEN WANT YOU TO CRACK IT.
RIGHT, TOMMY?
HM?
I SAID, LUCKY FOR US, WE'VE GOT BEDORE. HE, LIKE, DOESN'T EVEN BELIEVE IN TESTS.
OH. RIGHT. YEAH...LUCKY FOR US.
ARE YOU OKAY, DUDE? YOU'RE LOOKING A LITTLE, UH, YOU KNOW... GREEN.
LIKE, FOR REAL.
OH, YEAH. I'M ALL GOOD.
TOMMY--
I'LL CATCH UP WITH YOU GUYS LATER, COOL?

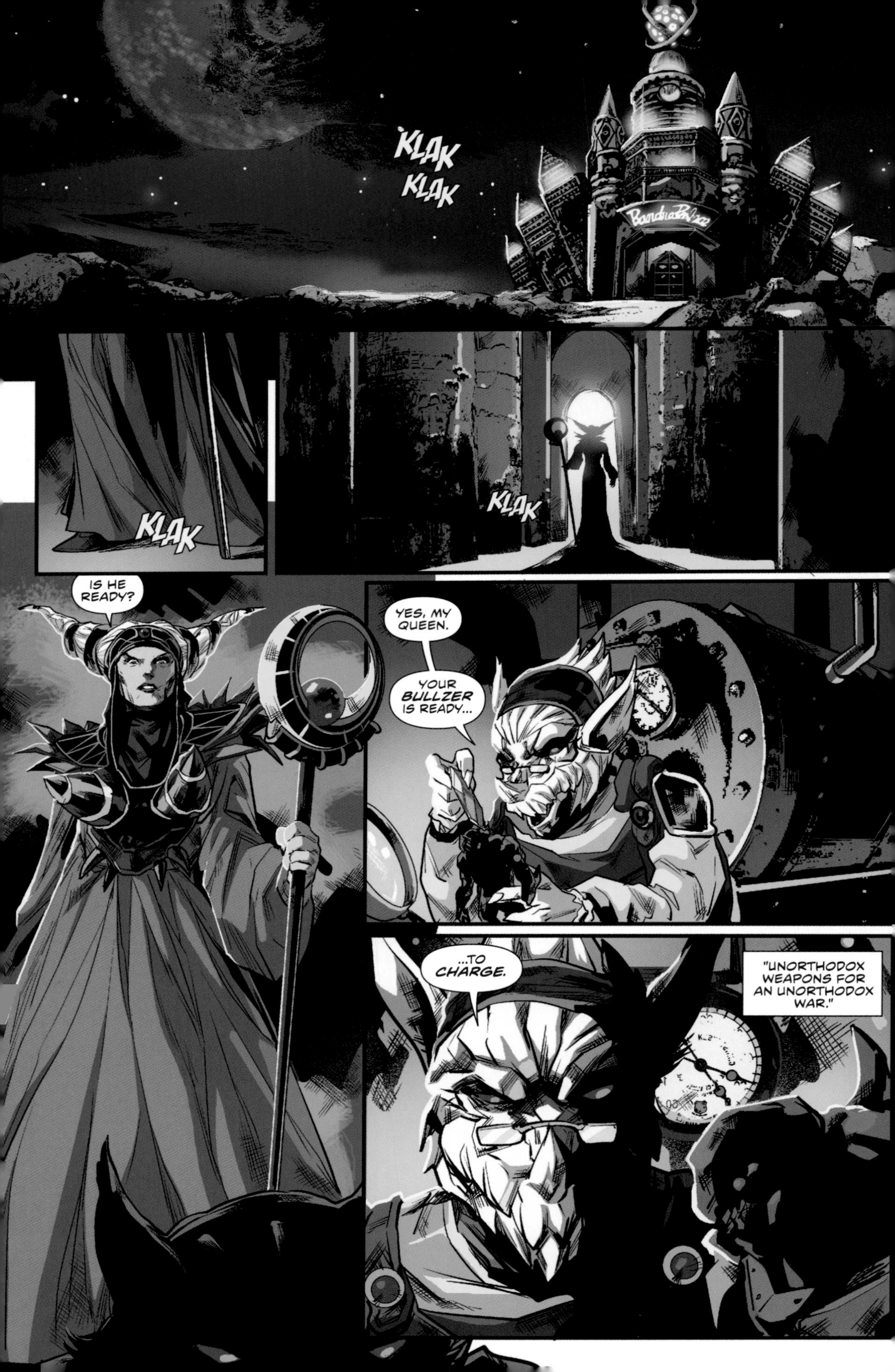
KLAK
KLAK
KLAK
KLAK
IS HE READY?
YES, MY QUEEN.
YOUR BULLZER IS READY...
...TO CHARGE.
"UNORTHODOX WEAPONS FOR AN UNORTHODOX WAR."

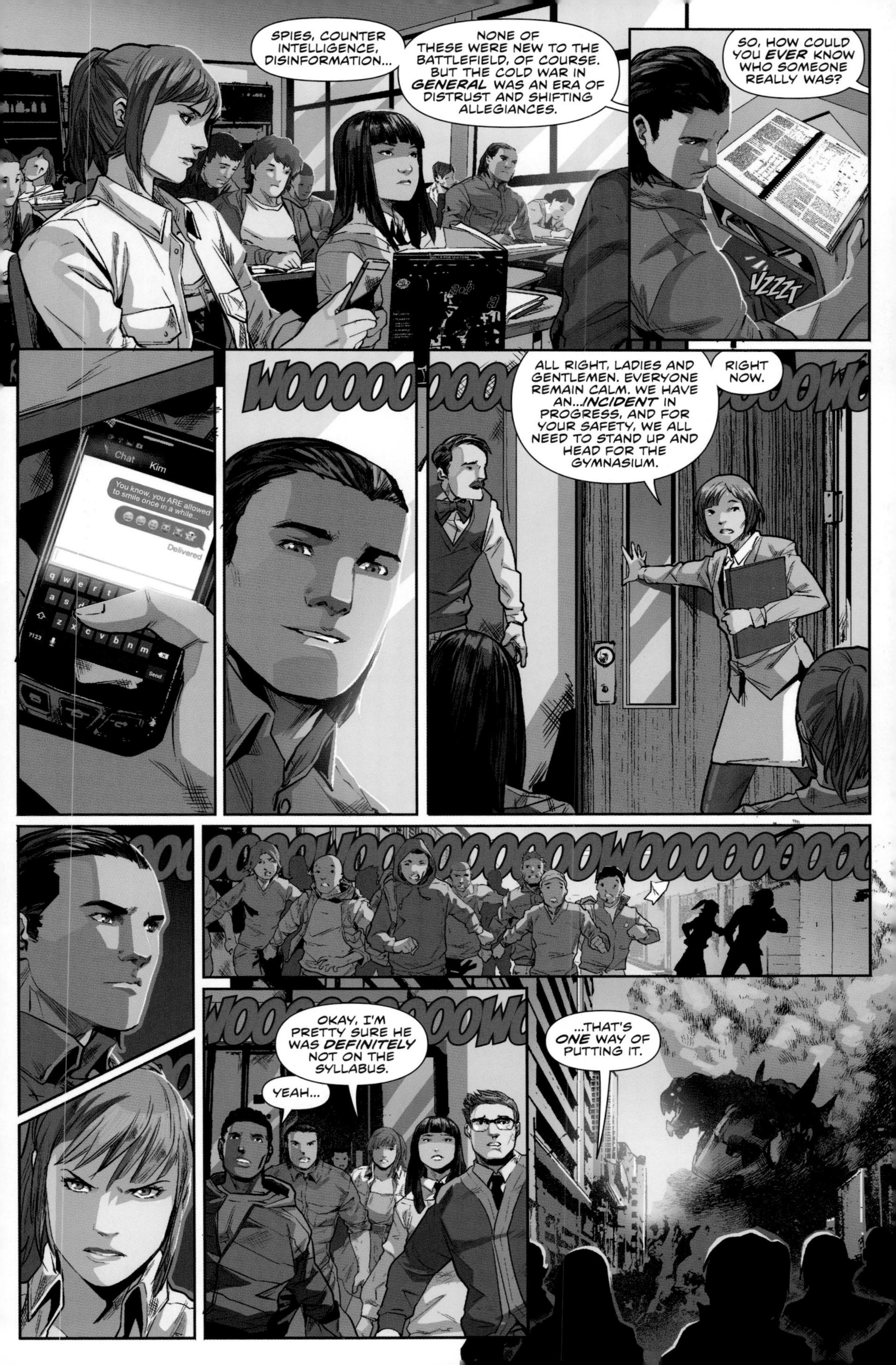
SPIES, COUNTER INTELLIGENCE, DISINFORMATION...
NONE OF THESE WERE NEW TO THE BATTLEFIELD, OF COURSE. BUT THE COLD WAR IN GENERAL WAS AN ERA OF DISTRUST AND SHIFTING ALLEGIANCES.
SO, HOW COULD YOU EVER KNOW WHO SOMEONE REALLY WAS?
VZZZT
Chat
Kim
You know, you ARE allowed to smile once in a while...
Delivered
Send
WOOOOOOOOOOOOWO
ALL RIGHT, LADIES AND GENTLEMEN. EVERYONE REMAIN CALM. WE HAVE AN...INCIDENT IN PROGRESS, AND FOR YOUR SAFETY, WE ALL NEED TO STAND UP AND HEAD FOR THE GYMNASIUM.
RIGHT NOW.
OOOWOOOOOOOOOOOWOOOOOOOOO
WOOOOOOOOOOWO
OKAY, I'M PRETTY SURE HE WAS DEFINITELY NOT ON THE SYLLABUS.
YEAH...
...THAT'S ONE WAY OF PUTTING IT.

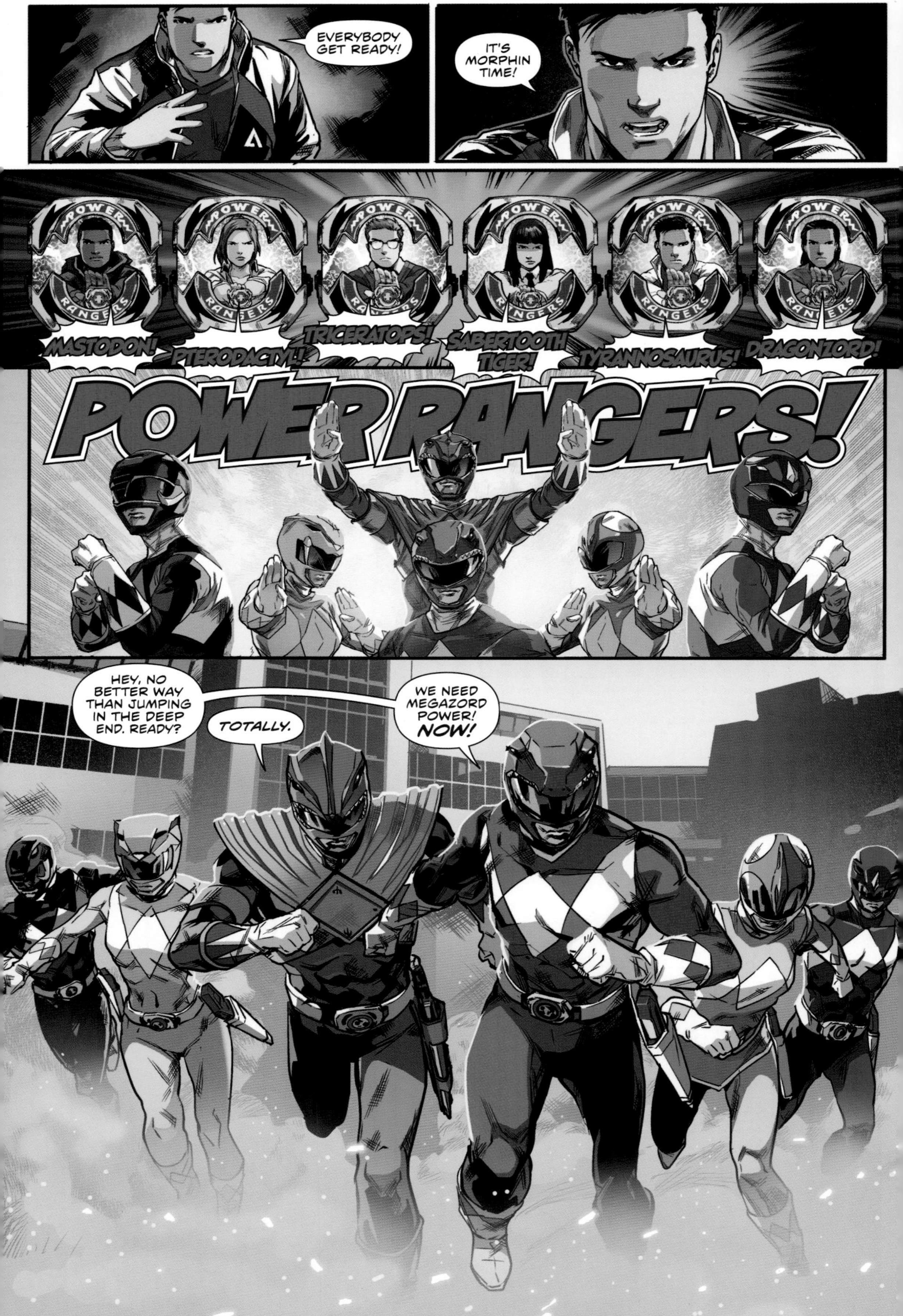
EVERYBODY GET READY!
IT'S MORPHIN TIME!
POWER
RANGERS
MASTODON!
PTERODACTYL!
TRICERATOPS!
SABERTOOTH TIGER!
TYRANNOSAURUS!
DRAGONZORD!
POWER RANGERS!
HEY, NO BETTER WAY THAN JUMPING IN THE DEEP END. READY?
TOTALLY.
WE NEED MEGAZORD POWER! NOW!

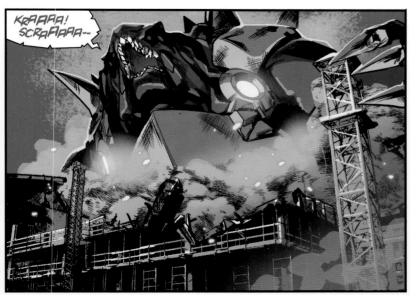

KRAAAA!
SCRAAAA--

--AAAA?

KA-SCRAAA!

KA--

THWOOOM

MAYBE THIS
IS A STUPID
QUESTION...

...BUT DO WE
HAVE ANY IDEA
WHAT THIS
THING IS?

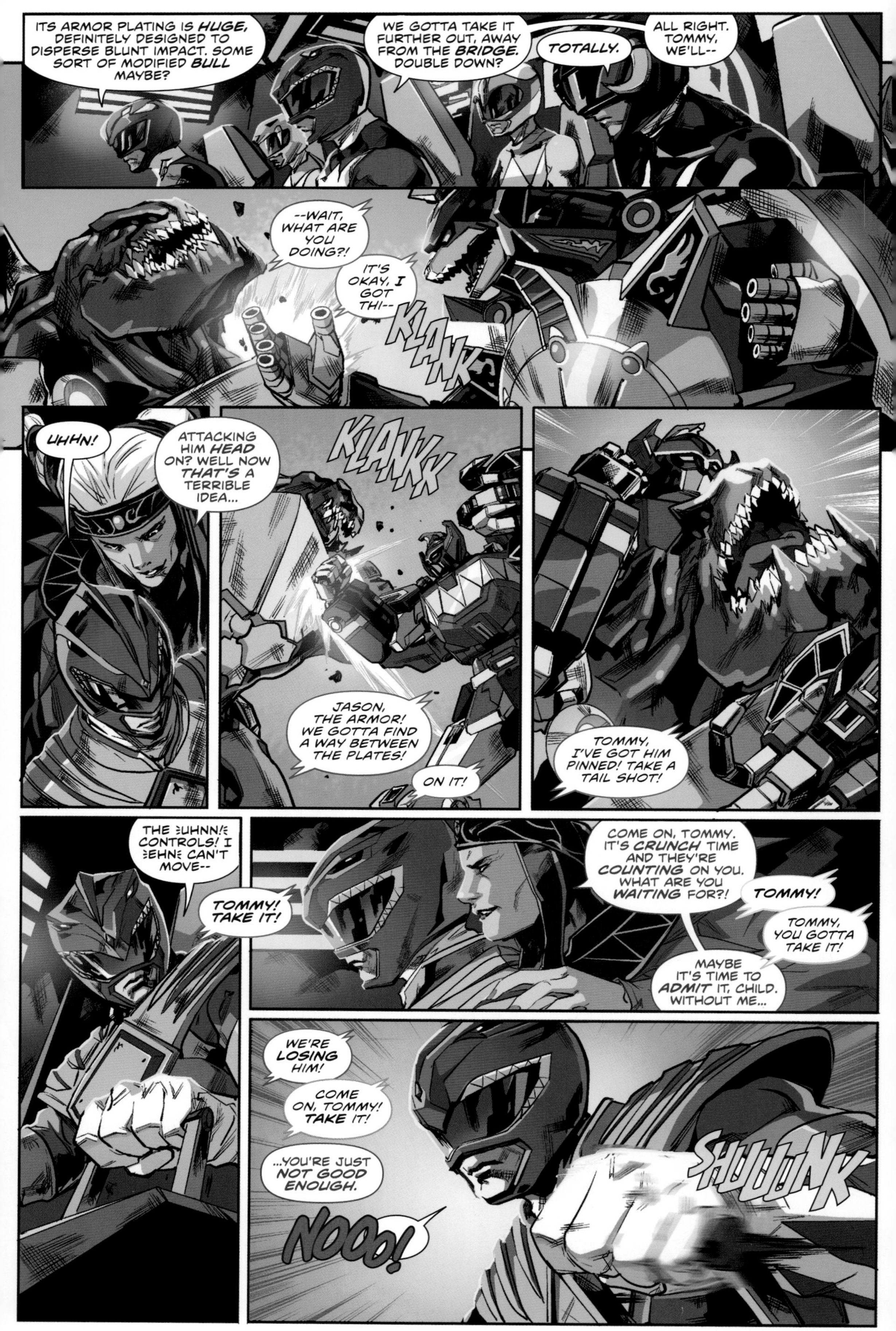

ITS ARMOR PLATING IS HUGE, DEFINITELY DESIGNED TO DISPERSE BLUNT IMPACT. SOME SORT OF MODIFIED BULL MAYBE?
WE GOTTA TAKE IT FURTHER OUT, AWAY FROM THE BRIDGE. DOUBLE DOWN?
TOTALLY.
ALL RIGHT. TOMMY, WE'LL--
--WAIT, WHAT ARE YOU DOING?!
IT'S OKAY, I GOT THI--
KLANK
UHHN!
ATTACKING HIM HEAD ON? WELL NOW THAT'S A TERRIBLE IDEA...
KLANKK
JASON, THE ARMOR! WE GOTTA FIND A WAY BETWEEN THE PLATES!
ON IT!
TOMMY, I'VE GOT HIM PINNED! TAKE A TAIL SHOT!
THE UHNN! CONTROLS! I EHN CAN'T MOVE--
TOMMY! TAKE IT!
COME ON, TOMMY. IT'S CRUNCH TIME AND THEY'RE COUNTING ON YOU. WHAT ARE YOU WAITING FOR?!
TOMMY!
TOMMY, YOU GOTTA TAKE IT!
MAYBE IT'S TIME TO ADMIT IT, CHILD. WITHOUT ME...
WE'RE LOSING HIM!
COME ON, TOMMY! TAKE IT!
...YOU'RE JUST NOT GOOD ENOUGH.
SHUUNK
NOOO!

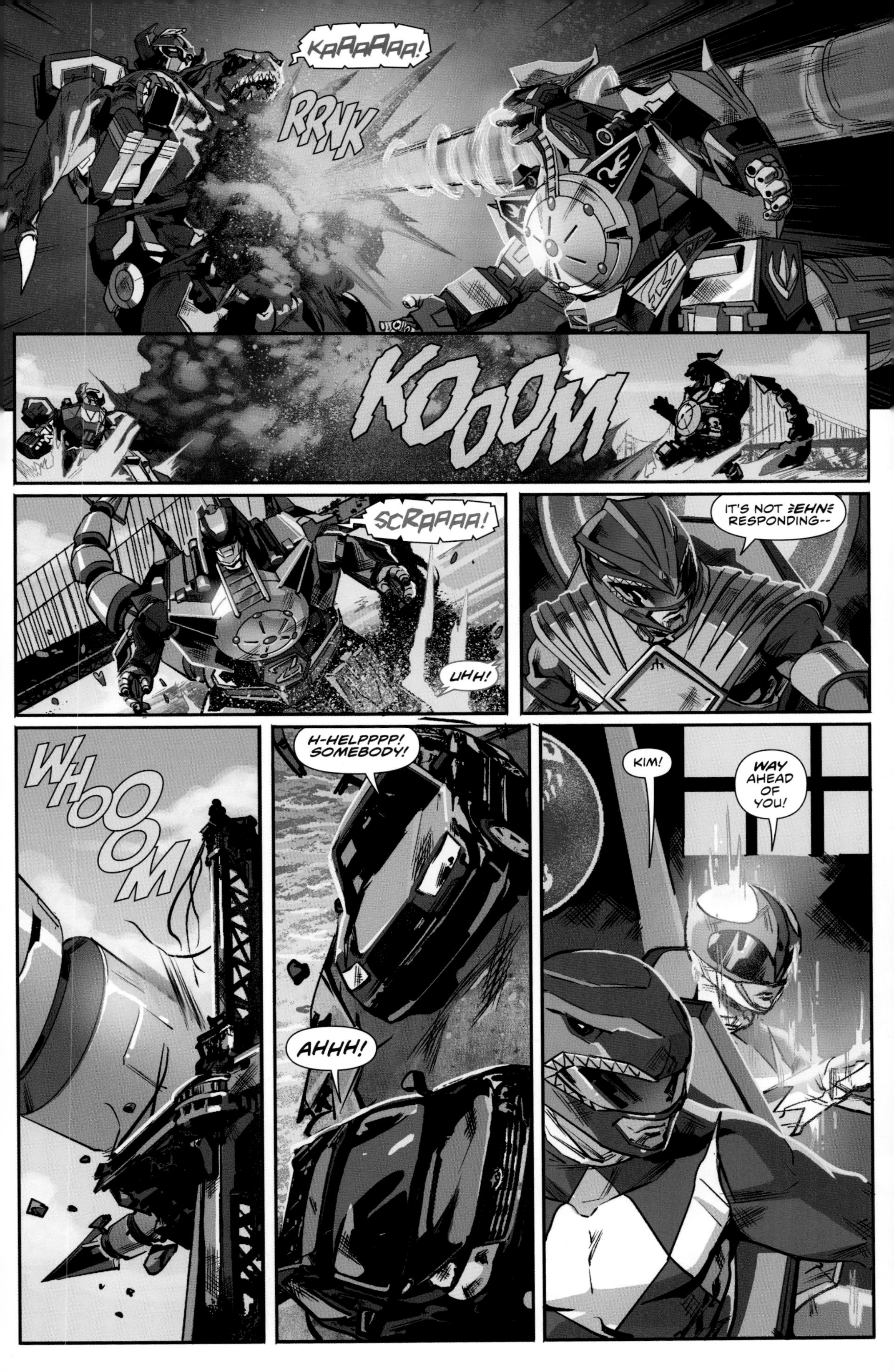
KAAAAAA!
RRNK
KOOOM
SCRAAAA!
UHH!
IT'S NOT *EHN* RESPONDING--
WHOOOM
H-HELPPPP! SOMEBODY!
AHHH!
KIM!
WAY AHEAD OF YOU!

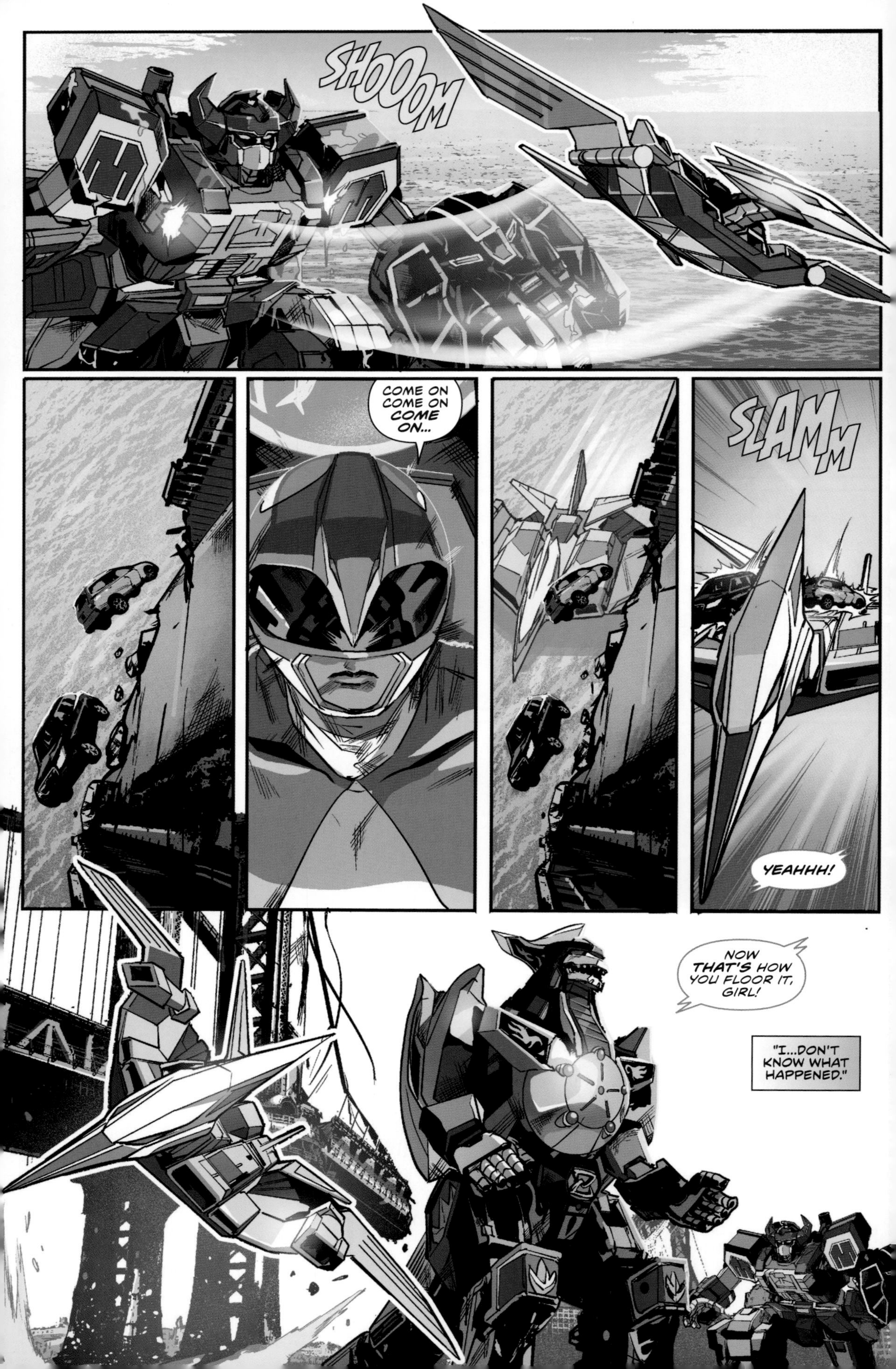
SHOOOM
COME ON COME ON COME ON...
SLAMMM
YEAHHH!
NOW THAT'S HOW YOU FLOOR IT, GIRL!
"I...DON'T KNOW WHAT HAPPENED."

THE DRAGONZORD CONTROLS JUST... *FROZE.*

I MEAN, I DON'T KNOW IF IT'S A WIRING GLITCH, OR WHAT--

--BUT MAYBE ALPHA CAN RUN SOME TESTS OR SOMETHING? I CAN'T BE OUT THERE WITH A FAULTY *ZORD.*

OR IF YOU CAN'T FOLLOW DIRECTIONS.

WHAT'S *THAT* SUPPOSED TO MEAN?

YOU DIDN'T LISTEN, MAN. THERE WAS A *PLAN*--

I HAVE NO IDEA WHAT "DOUBLE DOWN" EVEN *MEANS.*

YOU *PUT* THE BRIDGE AT RISK, AND ALL THOSE PEOPLE--

HEY, *YOU'RE* THE ONE THAT--

RANGERS. *PLEASE.*

JASON, AS TEAM LEADER, IT'S YOUR RESPONSIBILITY TO MAKE SURE EVERYONE HAS A CLEAR UNDERSTANDING OF OPERATING TACTICS AND PROCEDURES.

TOMMY, AS THE NEWEST MEMBER OF THE TEAM, IT'S *YOUR* RESPONSIBILITY TO ASK *QUESTIONS* WHEN YOU'RE UNCLEAR.

DO YOU BOTH UNDERSTAND?

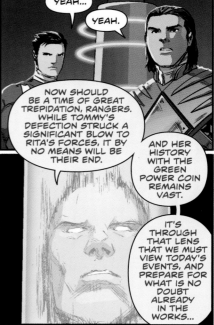

YEAH...

YEAH.

NOW SHOULD BE A TIME OF GREAT TREPIDATION, RANGERS. WHILE TOMMY'S DEFECTION STRUCK A SIGNIFICANT BLOW TO RITA'S FORCES, IT BY NO MEANS WILL BE THEIR END.

AND HER HISTORY WITH THE GREEN POWER COIN REMAINS VAST.

IT'S THROUGH THAT LENS THAT WE MUST VIEW TODAY'S EVENTS, AND PREPARE FOR WHAT IS NO DOUBT ALREADY IN THE WORKS...

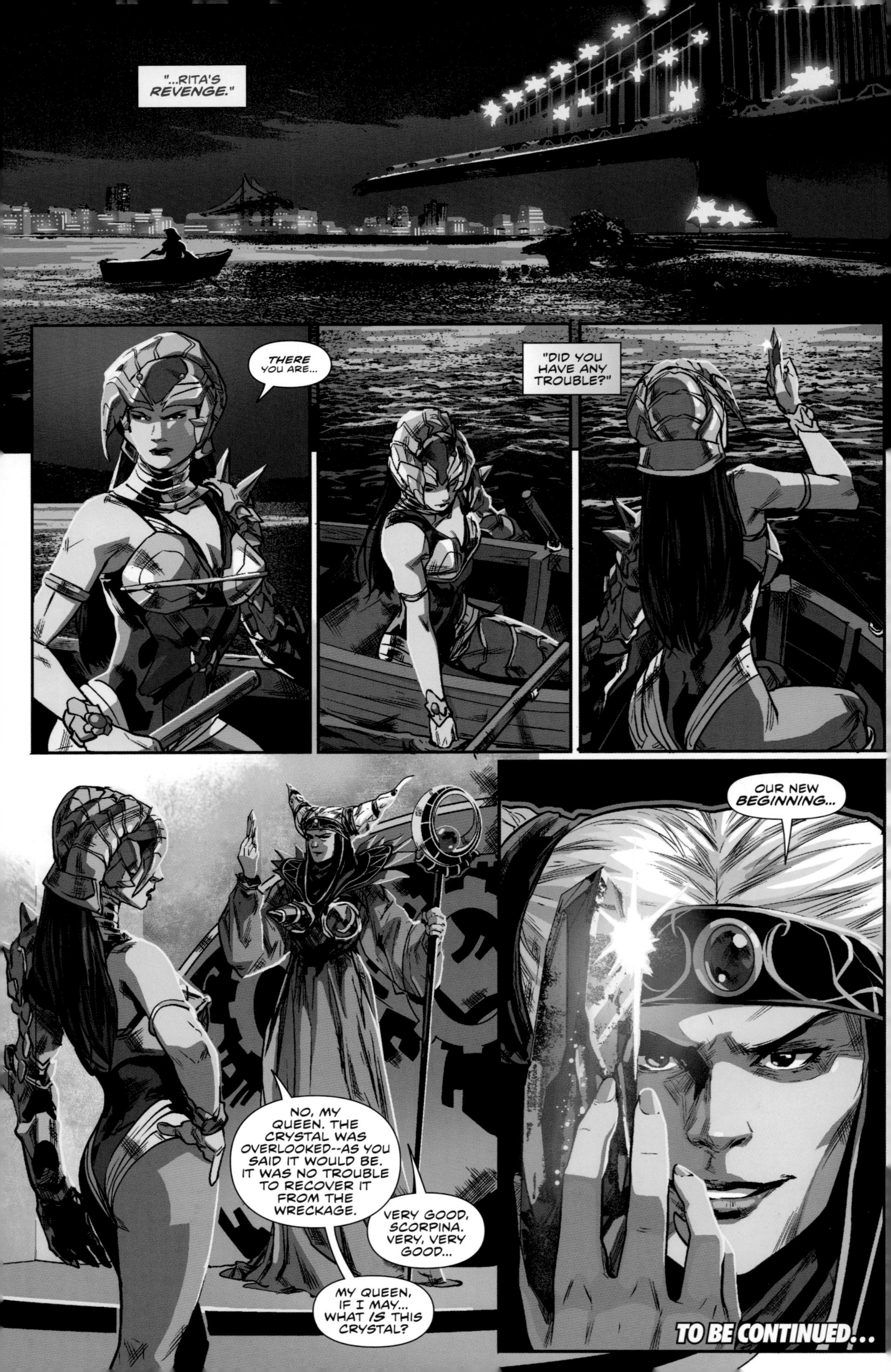
"...RITA'S REVENGE."
THERE YOU ARE...
"DID YOU HAVE ANY TROUBLE?"
NO, MY QUEEN. THE CRYSTAL WAS OVERLOOKED--AS YOU SAID IT WOULD BE. IT WAS NO TROUBLE TO RECOVER IT FROM THE WRECKAGE.
VERY GOOD, SCORPINA. VERY, VERY GOOD...
MY QUEEN, IF I MAY... WHAT IS THIS CRYSTAL?
OUR NEW BEGINNING...
TO BE CONTINUED...

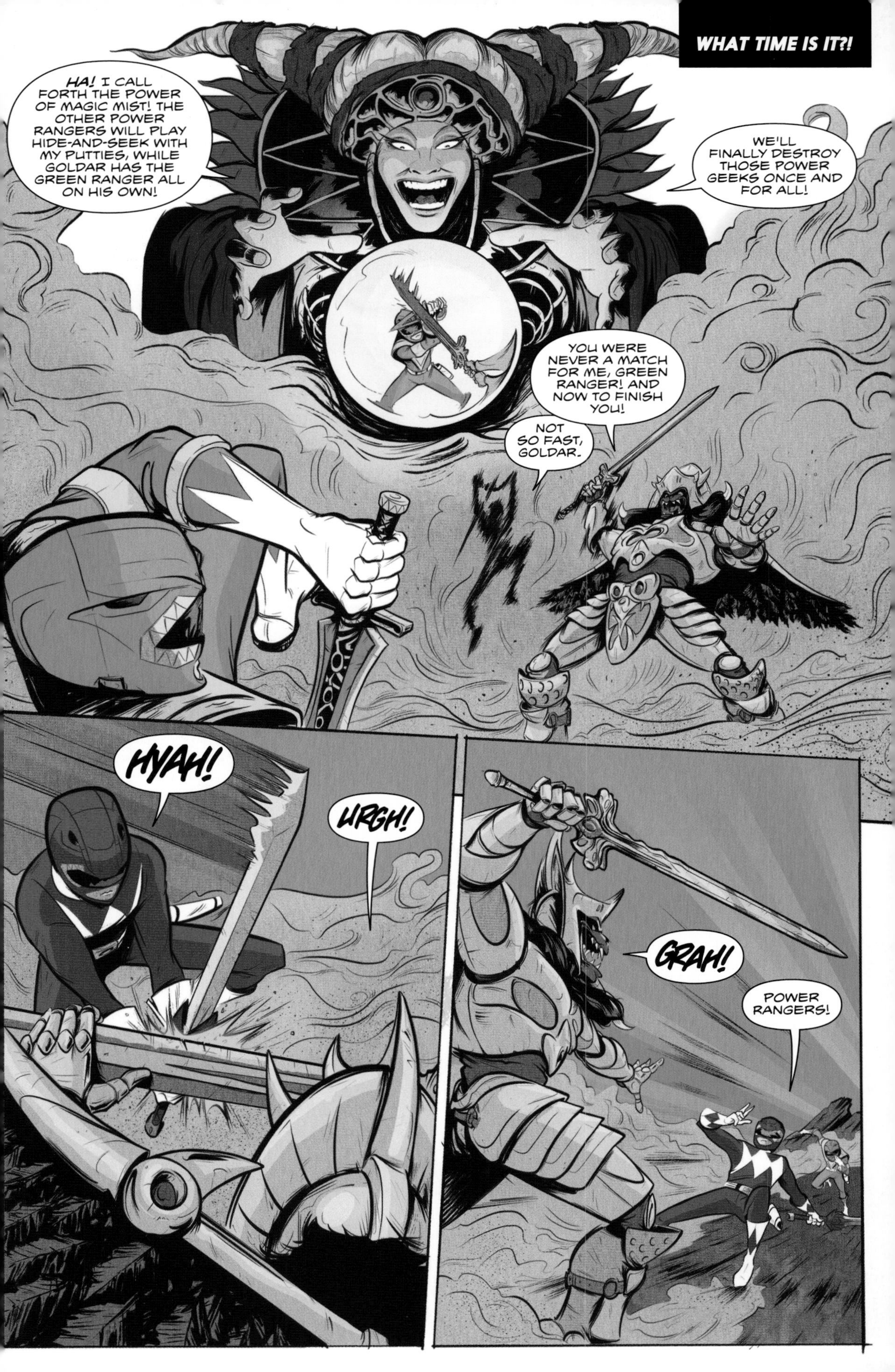
WHAT TIME IS IT?!
HA! I CALL FORTH THE POWER OF MAGIC MIST! THE OTHER POWER RANGERS WILL PLAY HIDE-AND-SEEK WITH MY PUTTIES, WHILE GOLDAR HAS THE GREEN RANGER ALL ON HIS OWN!
WE'LL FINALLY DESTROY THOSE POWER GEEKS ONCE AND FOR ALL!
YOU WERE NEVER A MATCH FOR ME, GREEN RANGER! AND NOW TO FINISH YOU!
NOT SO FAST, GOLDAR.
HYAH!
URGH!
GRAH!
POWER RANGERS!

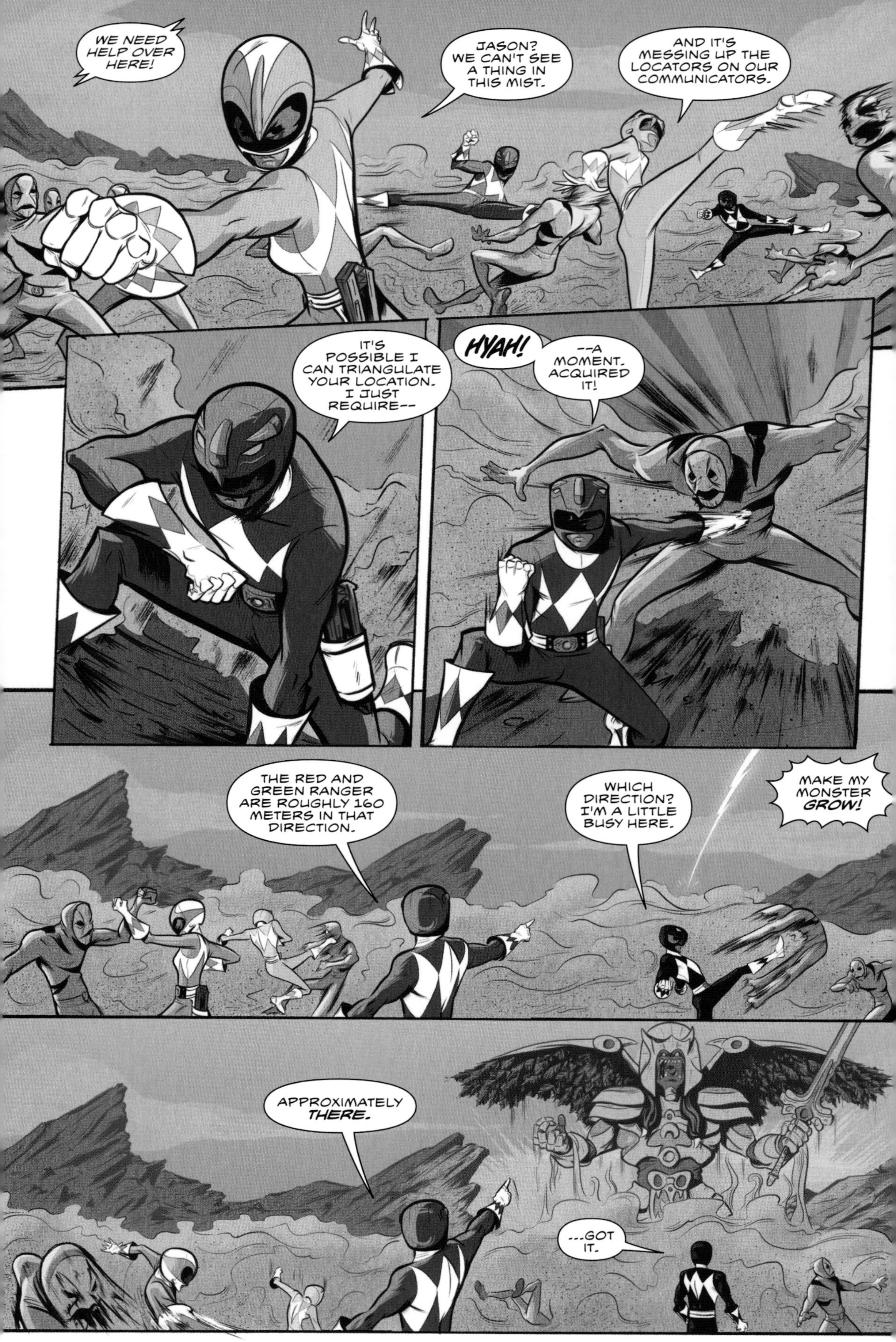
WE NEED HELP OVER HERE!
JASON? WE CAN'T SEE A THING IN THIS MIST.
AND IT'S MESSING UP THE LOCATORS ON OUR COMMUNICATORS.
IT'S POSSIBLE I CAN TRIANGULATE YOUR LOCATION. I JUST REQUIRE--
HYAH!
--A MOMENT. ACQUIRED IT!
THE RED AND GREEN RANGER ARE ROUGHLY 160 METERS IN THAT DIRECTION.
WHICH DIRECTION? I'M A LITTLE BUSY HERE.
MAKE MY MONSTER *GROW!*
APPROXIMATELY *THERE.*
...GOT IT.

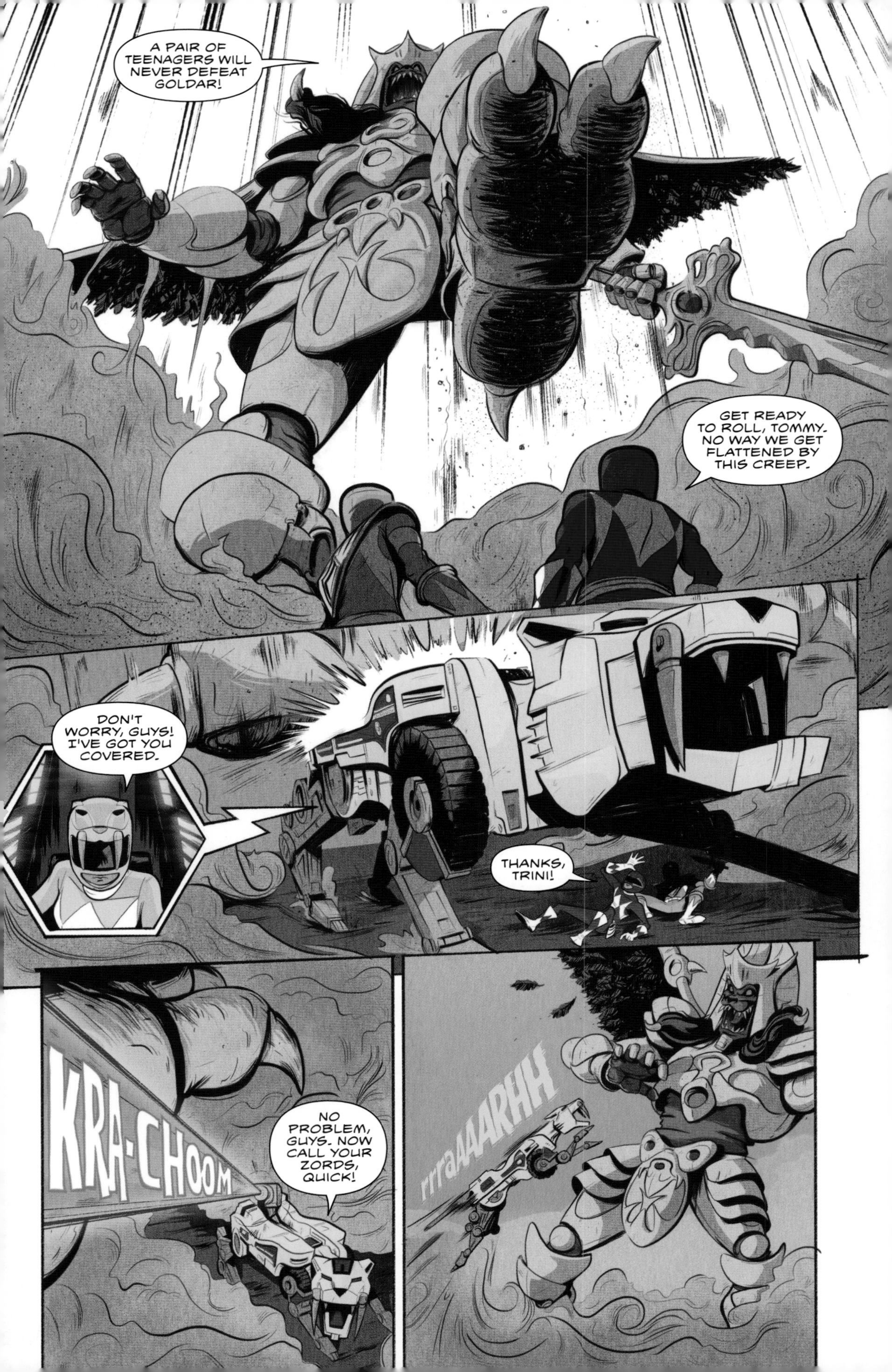
A PAIR OF TEENAGERS WILL NEVER DEFEAT GOLDAR!
GET READY TO ROLL, TOMMY. NO WAY WE GET FLATTENED BY THIS CREEP.
DON'T WORRY, GUYS! I'VE GOT YOU COVERED.
THANKS, TRINI!
KRA-CHOOM
NO PROBLEM, GUYS. NOW CALL YOUR ZORDS, QUICK!
rrraAAARHH

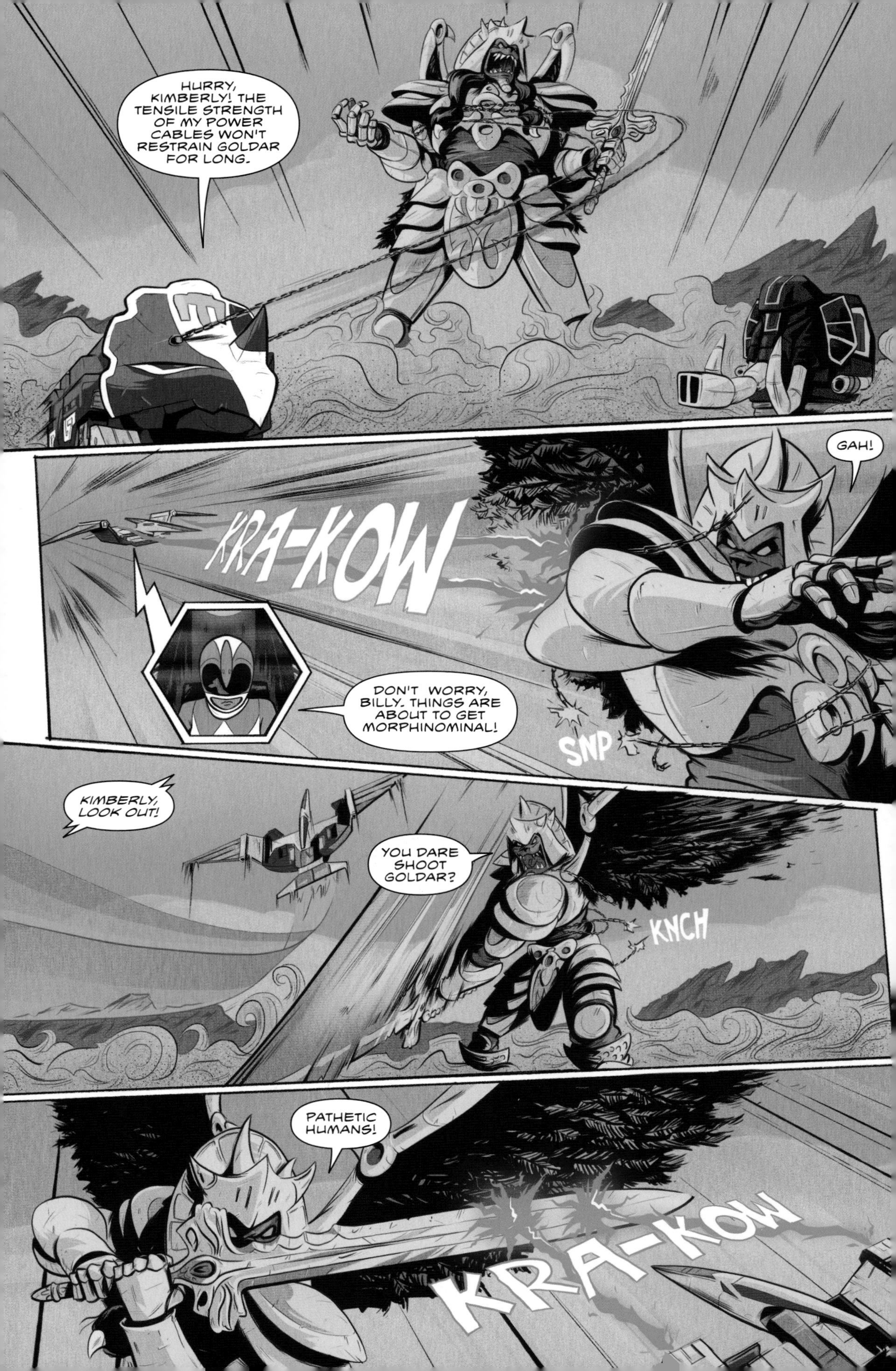
HURRY, KIMBERLY! THE TENSILE STRENGTH OF MY POWER CABLES WON'T RESTRAIN GOLDAR FOR LONG.
KRA-KOW
GAH!
DON'T WORRY, BILLY. THINGS ARE ABOUT TO GET MORPHINOMINAL!
SNP
KIMBERLY, LOOK OUT!
YOU DARE SHOOT GOLDAR?
KNCH
PATHETIC HUMANS!
KRA-KOW

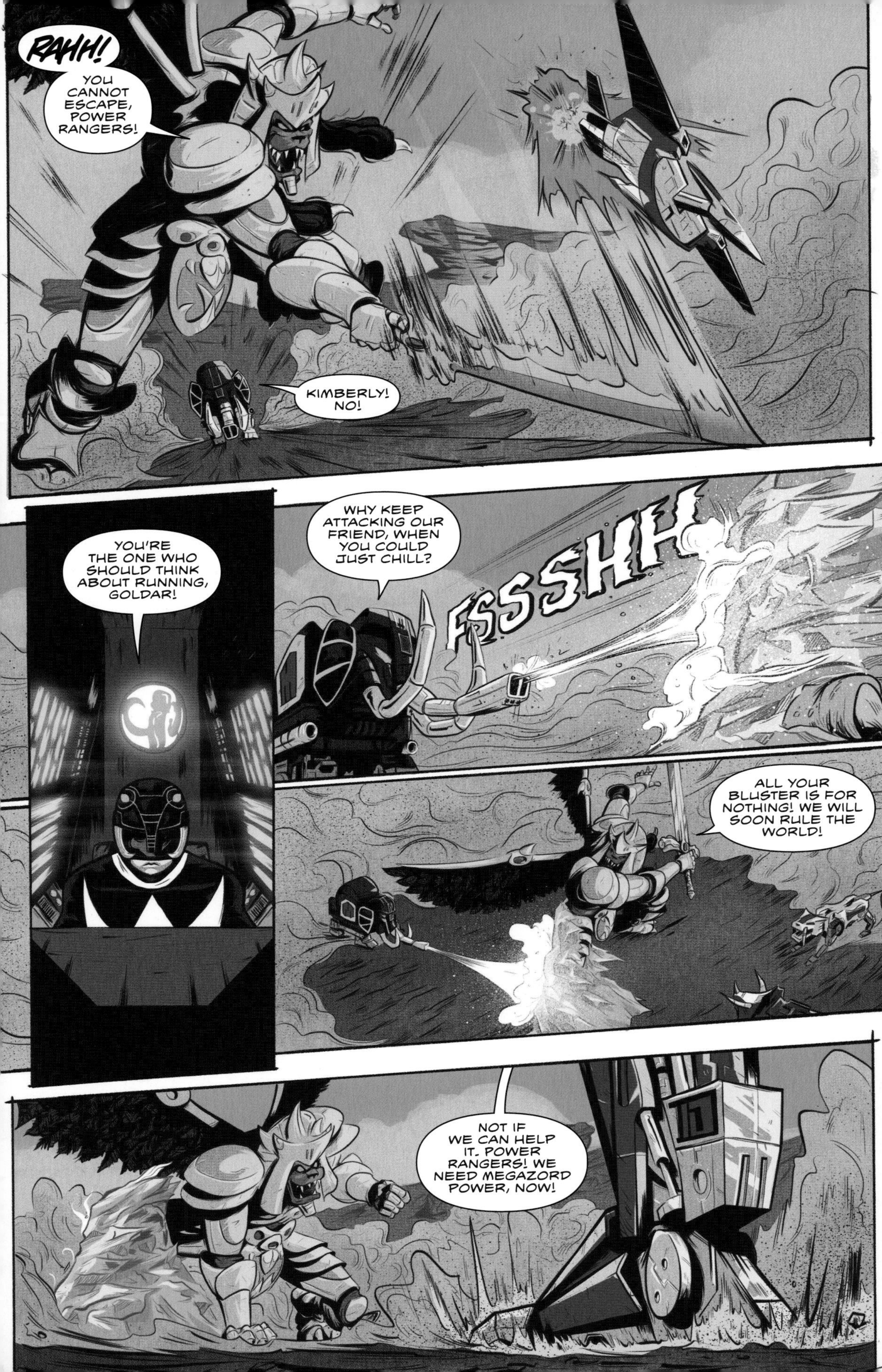
RAHH!
YOU CANNOT ESCAPE, POWER RANGERS!
KIMBERLY! NO!
YOU'RE THE ONE WHO SHOULD THINK ABOUT RUNNING, GOLDAR!
WHY KEEP ATTACKING OUR FRIEND, WHEN YOU COULD JUST CHILL?
FSSSHH
ALL YOUR BLUSTER IS FOR NOTHING! WE WILL SOON RULE THE WORLD!
NOT IF WE CAN HELP IT. POWER RANGERS! WE NEED MEGAZORD POWER, NOW!

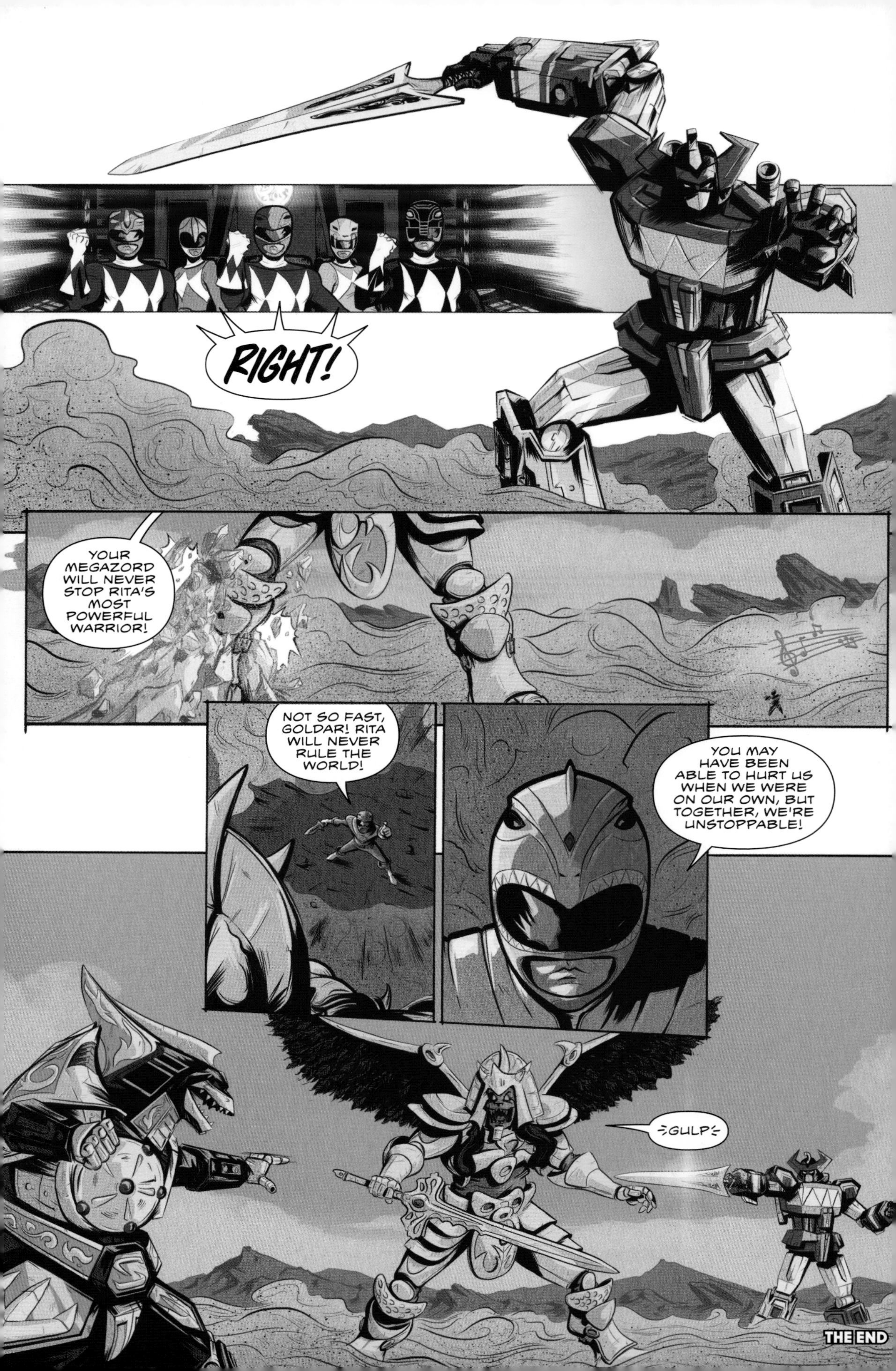
RIGHT!
YOUR MEGAZORD WILL NEVER STOP RITA'S MOST POWERFUL WARRIOR!
NOT SO FAST, GOLDAR! RITA WILL NEVER RULE THE WORLD!
YOU MAY HAVE BEEN ABLE TO HURT US WHEN WE WERE ON OUR OWN, BUT TOGETHER, WE'RE UNSTOPPABLE!
GULP
THE END

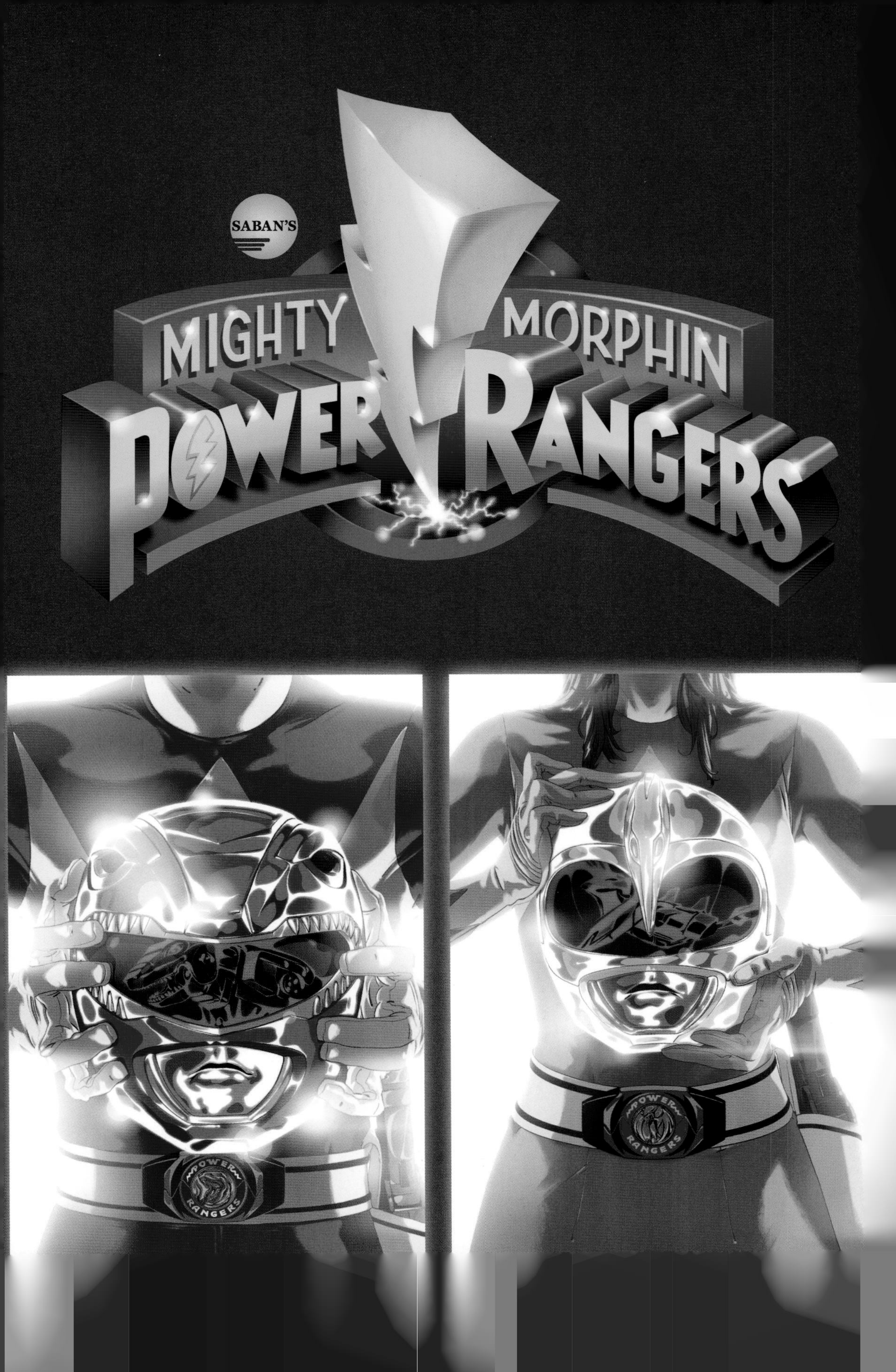
SABAN'S
MIGHTY MORPHIN
POWER RANGERS

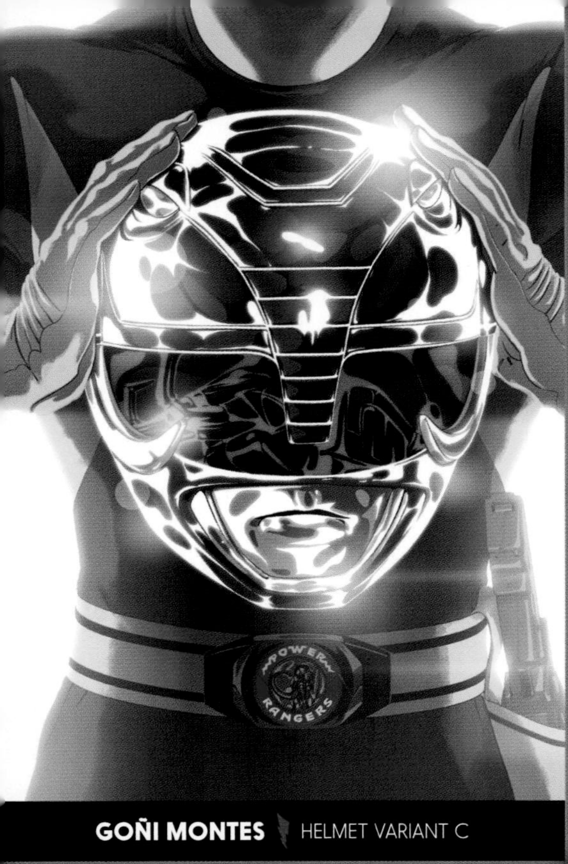
POWER RANGERS
GOÑI MONTES HELMET VARIANT C

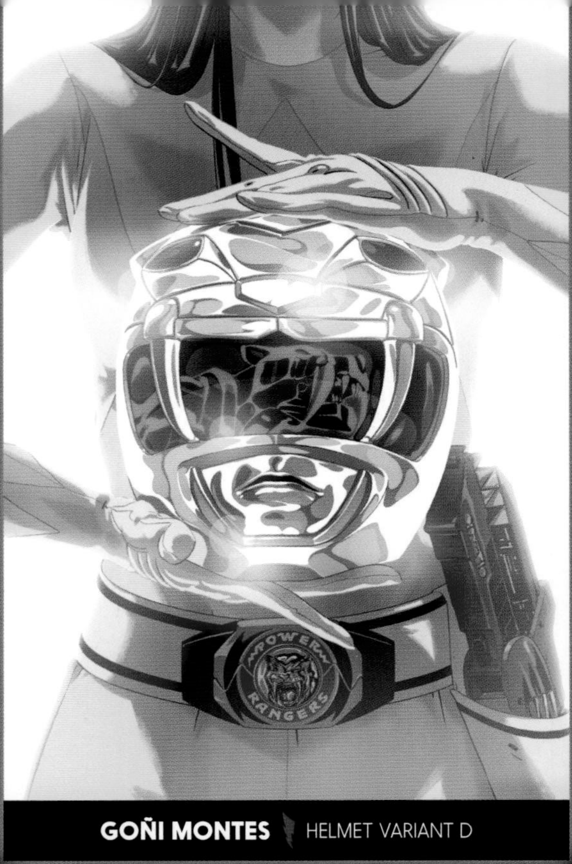
POWER RANGERS
GOÑI MONTES HELMET VARIANT D

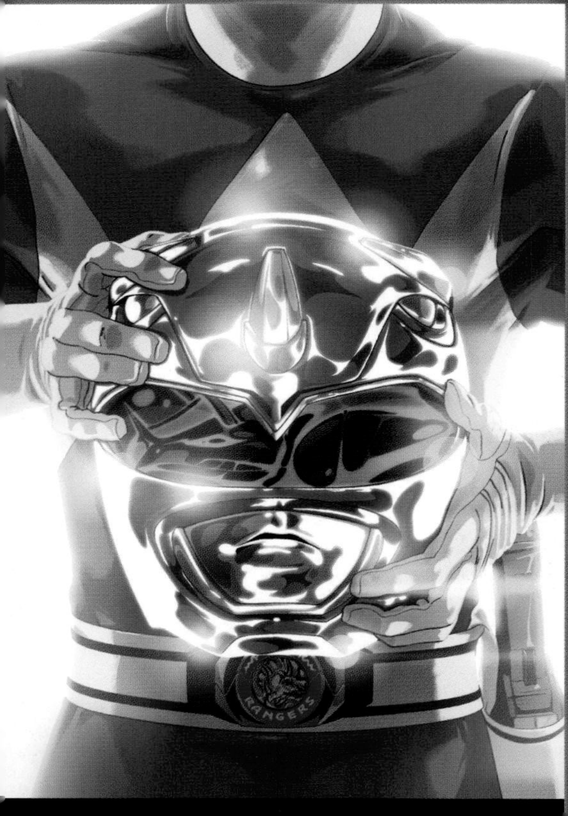
RANGERS

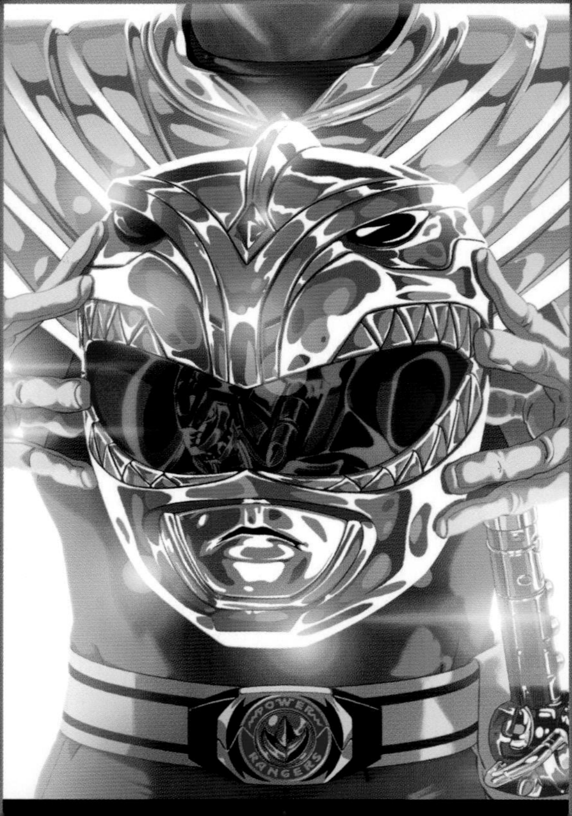
POWER RANGERS

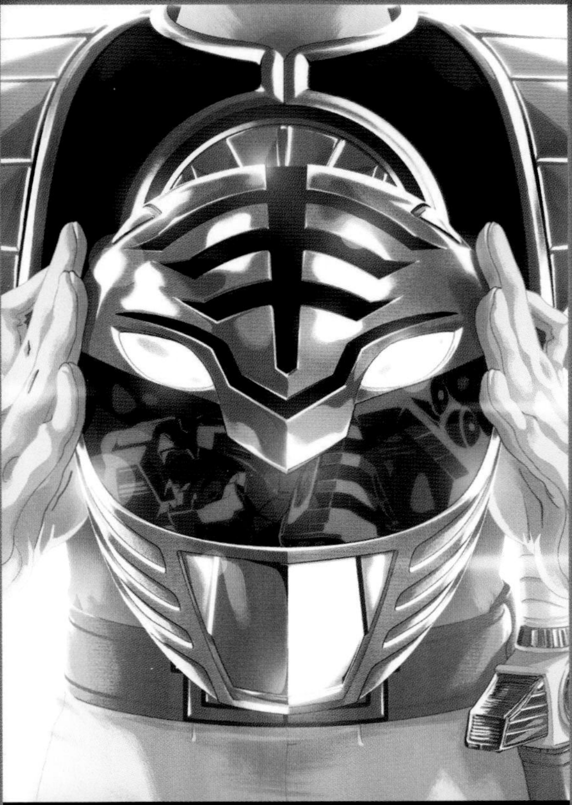

GOÑI MONTES HELMET VARIANT G

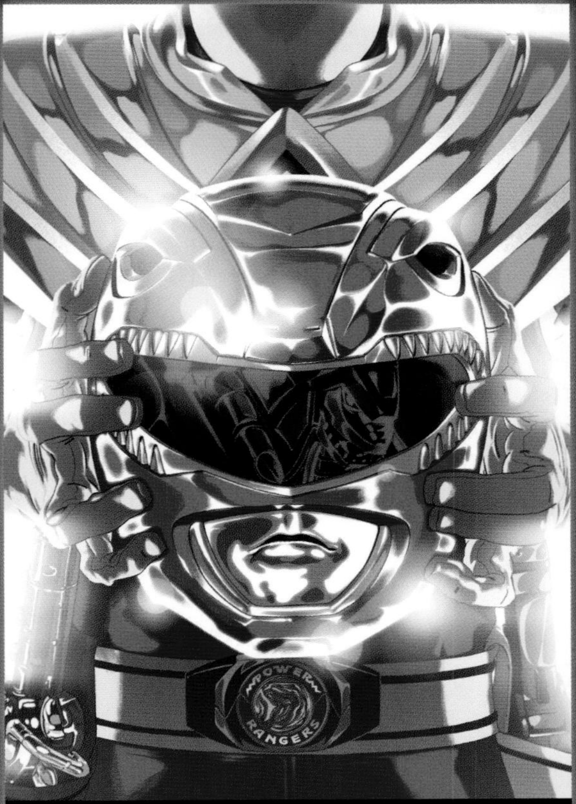
POWER
RANGERS

GOÑI MONTES HELMET VARIANT H

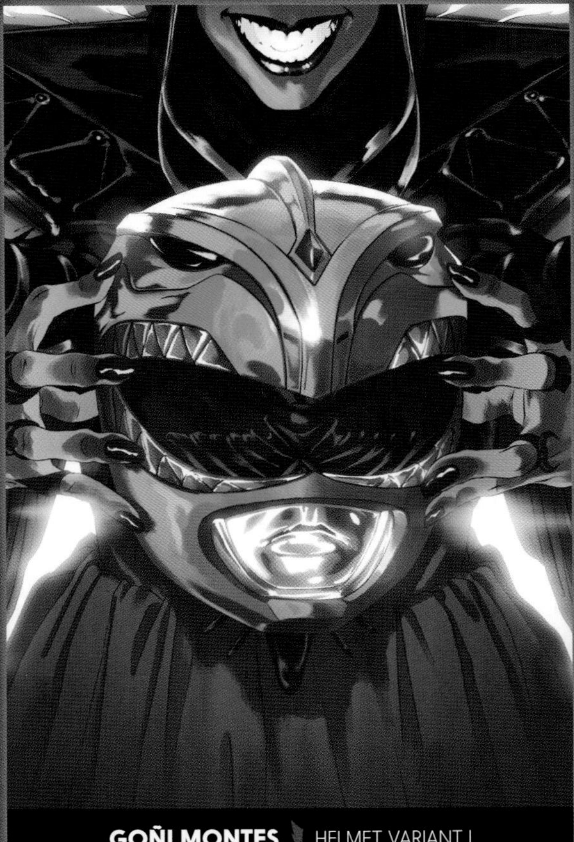

GOÑI MONTES HELMET VARIANT I

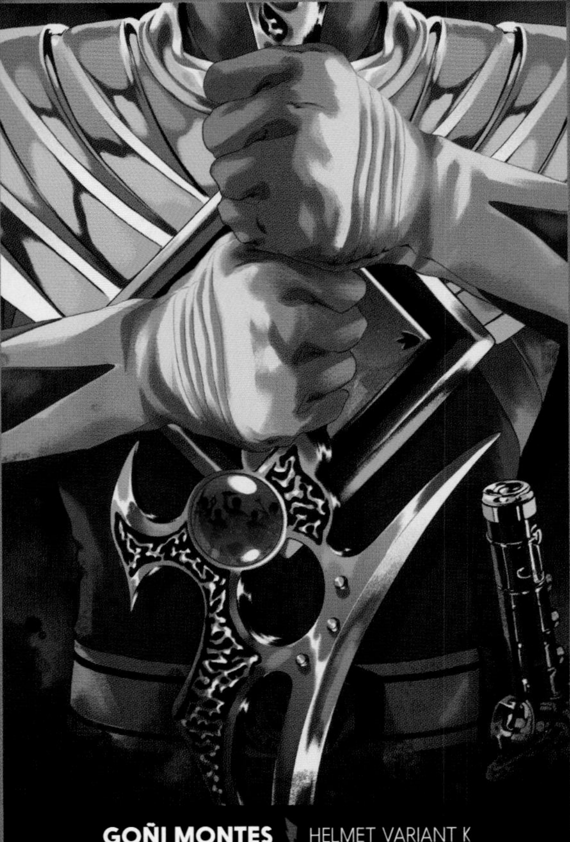

GOÑI MONTES HELMET VARIANT K

COLLECT THEM ALL!

Set of 9 Hardcover Books ISBN: 978-1-5321-4422-6

Hardcover Book ISBN
978-1-5321-4423-3

Hardcover Book ISBN
978-1-5321-4424-0

Hardcover Book ISBN
978-1-5321-4425-7

Hardcover Book ISBN
978-1-5321-4426-4

Hardcover Book ISBN
978-1-5321-4427-1

Hardcover Book ISBN
978-1-5321-4428-8

Hardcover Book ISBN
978-1-5321-4429-5

Hardcover Book ISBN
978-1-5321-4430-1

Hardcover Book ISBN
978-1-5321-4431-8